Stitch Crashes Disney

Written by PHAEA CREDE Illustrated by STEPH LABERIS

SCHOLASTIC
SYDNEY AUCKLAND NEW YORK TORONTO LONDON MEXICO CITY
NEW DELHI HONG KONG BUENOS AIRES PUERTO RICO

To Ms. Griffin, who taught me how to read and write. —P.C.

For Kiera, with love from Auntie Steph! —Steph Laberis

Published by Scholastic Australia in 2023.

Scholastic Australia Pty Limited
PO Box 579 Gosford NSW 2250
ABN 11 000 614 577
www.scholastic.com.au

Part of the Scholastic Group
Sydney • Auckland • New York • Toronto • London • Mexico City • New Delhi
Hong Kong • Buenos Aires • Puerto Rico

ISBN 978-1-76129-564-5

Printed in China.

Scholastic Australia's policy, in association with its printers, is to use papers that are renewable and made efficiently from wood grown in responsibly managed forests, so as to minimise its environmental footprint.

You, there! I need your help. I was supposed to take this blue alien—known as **Stitch**—back to my planet. But he ran away from me! Would you help find him before he causes too much trouble on Earth?

WANTED: STITCH

FOR BACKING UP SEWERS, REVERSING STREET SIGNS AND STEALING EVERYONE'S LEFT SHOE.

You will? Thank you! Keep your eyes peeled, and let's go!

First let's search this beach. Maybe ask that little mermaid and her friends if they've seen anything? But be speedy, before Stitch makes a big . . .

. . . Splash!

I told you he was tricky!
This is going to be harder than I thought.

Looks like these children have discovered a big secret: all you need to fly are happy thoughts and a bit of pixie dust! That's great for them, but your thoughts should be on Stitch. Where could he be hiding?

Yes! You found Stitch on the ceiling!
Now grab him before he gets away.

Wait . . . is that **pixie dust?**

Noooo!

Stitch is flying away.
We were so close!

Look at these three. No worries at all. Sure, we'd be *hakuna matata*-ing too if there wasn't a mischievous menace hiding in the jungle. Wait, what is Stitch doing with those vines?

Um, are you any good at untying knots?

Are my eyes tired from searching, or did that pumpkin become a carriage in one 'bibbidi-bobbidi-boo'? Well, we can't get distracted. Stitch is hiding around here, ready to cause more trouble.

Stitch, don't steal that woman's ride!

Bibbidi-bobbidi-bye!

10/6

Stitch is somewhere at this tea party—with all its tempting cookies and cakes. But don't stop for a snack, because I've heard these treats can cause some pretty **BIG** changes.

Don't let Stitch eat that cookie!

Now he's too big to catch! We'll have to wait
until the effects wear off on the next page.

Prince Ali sure has a lot of stuff. Golden camels. Purple peacocks. Persian monkeys! It's going to be impossible to find Stitch in this world-class menagerie.

Well, watch out, Stitch. Here we come!

And there he goes!

See those fancy outfits, that dim lighting and that singing teapot? We have to stop that sabotaging space creature from ruining the mood! Find Stitch quickly before something else happens.

Well. Something else happened.

I'm starting to think our mission
might not be a **smashing** success.

Is Stitch disguised as a clown?
An acrobat? A circus animal?
He could be anywhere!

This is intense! Get it? **In tents.**
Because we're in a tent!

You're right. This is no time for jokes.

MAIN
ENTRANCE

That's not what they mean by a

big finale!

That's it. I give up. Stitch is too slippery for us.
We might as well have one last meal before
we face the music. Excuse me, waiter?

Wait . . . does that waiter look familiar?

You naughty little catastrophe-causing,
mischief-making, rude blue dude!

Wait, what am I saying? We got him!
Now to get him on my spaceship.

Wait . . . who is that driving my ship?

STITCH!!!